I0601180

Navigating By Stars

Navigating By Stars

24 Very Short Stories of Love & Longing

Mark Russell Gelade

A Caveat Lector Book

REGENT PRESS
Berkeley, California

Copyright © 2018 by Mark Russell Gelade

[paperback]
ISBN 13: 978-1-58790-441-7
ISBN 10: 1-58790-441-1

[e-book]
ISBN 13: 978-1-58790-443-1
ISBN 10: 1-58790-443-8

Library of Congress Catalog Number: 2018941691

The characters and events in this book are fictitious.
Any reference to an actual place, any similarity to real
people, living or dead, is entirely coincidental
and not intended by the author.

Manufactured in the U.S.A.
REGENT PRESS
Berkeley, California
www.regentpress.net

Acknowledgements

The author wishes to thank the many readers and friends who have contributed editorial advice and guidance in shaping these stories, including: Phil Cousineau for his tough love and reverence for storytelling; Anne Dubuisson for her insightful manuscript review; Christopher Bernard and the Liar's Café crew for their camaraderie; and Robert Olen Butler, whose early affirmation and writing insights continue to inspire.

Several stories from this collection have previously appeared in: *Narrative Magazine; Fiction Attic; Southeast Review;* and *Synchronized Chaos.* Thanks also to *Glimmer Train* for the 2017, Very Short Fiction Honorable Mention.

My deep appreciation to Mark Weiman at Regent Press for his attentive care in the production and publication of this book. www.regentpress.com.

And finally, special thanks to my wife Colette, for her enduring love and support.

Table of Contents

Introduction

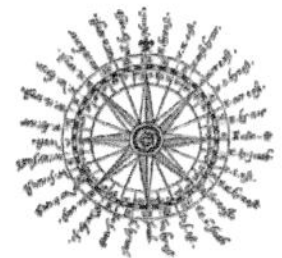

Navigating by Stars began life with a whisper of words spoken in my ear by a female voice, giving birth in the middle of a rainstorm so intense, it had washed out the local bridge, necessitating an unplanned home birth. That visitation became *The Bridge is Down*, and it was the first 'short short' I ever wrote.

Inhabiting a poet's sensibility by nature, I never considered myself a prose writer. Indeed, after the first draft of the *The Bridge is Down*, I was at a loss to weigh what I had written. It felt longer than a traditional prose poem and more character-focused than most flash fiction I had encountered.

It was not long after, while perusing a copy of Poets & Writers magazine, that I noticed a call for submissions for: *The World's Best Short, Short Story Contest*, sponsored by Florida State University (FSU) and judged by Pulitzer Prize-winning author, Robert Olen Butler.

Despite the grandiose contest name, or perhaps even

because of it, I was intrigued. The maximum word count for submissions was 500 words. I ran a word count on my new story and tightened it up to 460 words, then sent it in.

A few months later, while driving home from some errands, my cell phone rang. It was the FSU English Department saying that Robert Olen Butler had selected *The Bridge is Down* as the contest winner, and that he was eager to meet the woman who wrote the story! (I can offer no further explanation for how the female voices herein entered my psyche.)

First-person narratives are a mysterious thing. There is some strange magic involved, as a voice appears out of the ether and begins to speak. That is the precise moment when the writer's job is to step aside and listen. I practiced this, with moderate success, over a period of several years, until the current volume assembled.

There are patterns and some inter-relationships here, just barely perceptible among the stars. My hope is that you enjoy following these voices as they journey across the night sky.

Navigating by Stars

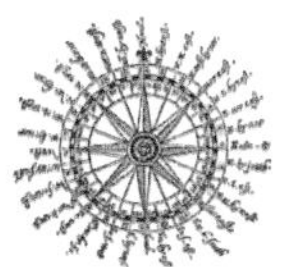

HARRY, Stan, and Peg, their names still legible on the wooden roadside memorial—looks like someone's left fresh flowers. One year ago to the day; they had headed down from Bolinas and across the Golden Gate Bridge to San Francisco to get tattoos and piercings.

Stan and Peg hadn't stopped talking about it all week— what they would get, where they would get it. Stan was thinking of going with something tribal, maybe an arm band or calf-band. Peg had settled on a crimson butterfly, angled slightly on her right shoulder. And Harry? Harry wasn't much interested in tattoos—he was thinking about getting his ear pierced, probably daydreaming about studs and rings.

That summer, they had each arrived at a turning point. Stan announced that he was done being a handyman and was finally going to get his Contractor's license. Peg was thinking about marrying Stan, though he hadn't asked her yet; and I think my brother Harry had finally made up his mind to leave Bolinas altogether, apply to college, and get his degree.

The phone had rung at an awkward hour, too late at night to be good news.

Stan was driving, Peg seated next to him, and then Harry, his head resting on his palm, probably gazing out the passenger window.

Winding back up the mountain road toward home, Stan had misjudged the curve, and with too little room for correction, the pickup had careened over the deep ravine and dropped down into the moonlit surf below—a skid mark arcing across the lanes like a black rainbow.

I was the one who had talked Harry into getting the piercing. I thought he could use a little something to spruce up his image—he'd been all gloom-and-doom lately.

I recommended a diamond stud, nothing outrageous, just a firm but understated emblem of his counterculture status. I actually thought it might help him a bit with the girls, since he wasn't breaking any records in that department either. Now the only broken record to speak of is the one that keeps running through my head whenever I can't fall asleep at night.

My dear brother, I tremble as the stars come out and night falls: you out there, falling through air, Peg's long hair lifting, fluttering against your face—the sudden absence of road noise.

And although the story of your brief life leads only to this gravel-dusted cross, etched with your name, I know you would have risen above the ravine as the truck went airborne.

You would have kept on going too, and not looked down. You would have fixed your green eyes steadfastly on the brightest star in the night sky and risen to meet it—just like any other future.

All That I Desire

THURSDAYS are when a group of us from work gathers for happy hour drinks. It's also the time when Grant and I get to flirt a little and 'test the limits.'

We're on our second round of Vodka tonics, and as usual, Grant is holding court. He's recounting another tale from the annals of our customer service desk at the high-end home improvement store where we all work.

Week in and week out, we deal with stressed-out interior designers and beleaguered homeowners who've chosen the 'go-it-alone' approach.

Every now and then, I catch Grant eyeing himself in the tinted mirror that runs the length of the bar. He has the weary good looks of the young man he used to be—a Triple-A baseball prospect—until a knee injury laid his professional baseball dreams to rest. I will say this in his defense—he still looks pretty good for a man his age, which is more than I can say for a lot of the guys I've dated recently.

The topic of conversation is Kyle Monroe, a high-maintenance interior designer who's a regular at our customer service counter. A moment later, we all break out in hysterics, and my hand gently lands on Grant's thigh and rests there for a moment.

I'm not sure I can say exactly what it is that I want from this flirtation, but I will admit that I crave Grant's attention. Of course, with a wife and kid, he's got a lot more at stake than I do, but why should I really care? I crave the feeling of being wanted.

It is beginning to grow dark outside and our small group is thinning out. I'm wondering whether this will be the night that Grant suggests we stay on for a bite to eat. Then, as if by reflex, I start to obsess on the size of my thighs and the diet that I know I'm supposed to start and how secretly, I don't feel so desirable.

I glance up at the blackboard above the bar. In colored chalk, it says a reggae band is scheduled to start playing at 9:00 p.m. I'm secretly calculating the odds of whether Grant will suggest dinner, and whether he will ask me to dance. He knows I love to dance.

I could dance myself right off the planet tonight, if only he were willing. Truthfully—if you asked me—to dance is sometimes all that I desire.

With His Own Eyes

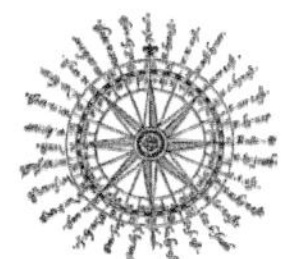

MR. FRANCESCA arrived at our front door on Sunday. I recognized him right away, despite his graying hair and the weather-beaten look he concealed beneath a jaunty San Francisco Giants baseball cap and matching windbreaker.

"George!" I said, extending a hand, "how *are* you?"

Mr. Francesca had owned this house for almost thirty years before we bought it from him last year. Back then, we had learned that his wife had recently passed away and he was selling up and moving to North Carolina to be closer to his daughter.

As first-time homeowners, we had been eager to make the place our own. We had embarked on a frenzy of home-improvement projects; and so I suppose it was not without some pride that I ushered Mr. Francesca in through the front door and offered him the grand tour.

He dutifully followed me first into the living room, then to the new kitchen, and then down the hallway, where we had opened up the ceiling and installed a new skylight.

But Mr. Francesca seemed unimpressed. I could sense his growing impatience as he glanced into each room, making a soft, snorting sound under his breath.

By the time we reached the back of the house, his exasperation was evident, and when he spotted the new French doors leading out to the garden, he made a beeline for open space and fresh air.

Mr. Francesca stood on the deck, leaning on the wooden handrail for support. Around his neck, a Saint Christopher medal dangled on a long gold chain that reflected the light of the sun in a blinding white light.

"She got that job down at Sears and worked full time— right up until she passed," he said, jabbing his thumb backwards over his shoulder.

I looked up at him and noticed the delicate muscles of his cheek twitching.

Then, from down in the garden, my wife turned and waved and offered a cautious 'Hi' to someone who at first she did not recognize.

"Honey," I called out, "you remember Mr. Francesca!?"

But Mr. Francesca was not looking back at her. He was staring at a point much farther off; seeing with his own eyes, the scalloped pink petals and tall, green stem of a wild ginger plant, growing defiantly from a bed of dry, sandy soil—many years ago—in the same place where now a tangle of star jasmine coiled across a new redwood fence.

"She loved ginger...." he said softly, and his eyes fluttered closed. And for a moment, everything in the garden grew still.

The Bridge is Down

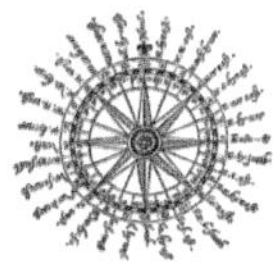

THE RAIN has been driving down for twelve straight hours. The radio says anyone on the flood plain should get ready to evacuate. The river is an angry torrent of mud, broken branches, and fractured limbs. Flash floods are pretty much the norm this time of year, but things will change after the storm—you just know it.

The contractions started last night, and I told Bill it was just my luck the heavens should burst open right about the same time I was going to. We've already settled on a name; if it's a girl, we'll call her Ginger, if it's a boy— William Jr.—after his dad.

Bill's got the route planned out. We'll head through town, across the bridge, past the post office, and on down US101.

Bill has a phone in one hand and the radio tucked under his arm; every minute or so he cranes his neck to glance back at me from across the hall.

The pain is pinning me down—pulling me to another place in my brain where I can smell wet earth and feel the heat of my own blood gushing through my veins.

Another pang, and a fine sheen of sweat forms on my forehead. The rain is falling with a deep drumming groan on the yard.

The ground is more liquid than land right now, and I'm thinking that at any minute the whole house will lift on a swell of water and float into town. I might lift and float slowly into town.

Bill worked at the local lumber mill until it closed down last year. We're "in transition," as they say. Only the little cosmic joke on us was that ready or not, we were pregnant.

"Bill," I call out, "shut the heater, I'm burning up here."

The body I used to know and understand is undergoing some seriously dark changes—deep roots twisting and pulling at me like a trunk being hauled out of the earth. My fists are clenching the sheets—my belly about as round as a planet.

"Bill, it's getting close, we gotta get going."

Then, hands through his hair, cupping the phone: "Honey," he tells me, "the bridge is down—we're gonna have to do this here."

There are enough people looking in on me now, you'd think this was some kind of circus attraction. Bill's mom is gripping my hand. The rain is pouring in from the ends of the earth, but it's my own water that is broken now.

There is water everywhere, inside and out, sweat and

rain and urine; and through it all, the only one among us who can breathe through water is coming blindly across its own bridge—coming out for air—crying out for air.

Vicentas, Maid

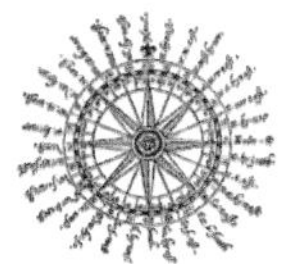

THAT QUICK left-right, left-right scraping of slippers across the concrete floor, and that out-of-breath huffing for air that you hear, belong to Vicentas, our maid, or I should say, the maid of Casa Grandé, the hacienda we rent each summer in Mexico—I cannot, for reasons that will become obvious, say which town exactly.

But there's a green parrot next door that knows the reason—knowledge he evidently acquired from the hours spent in his demented habit of knocking his green and orange head against the upstairs windowpane.

It has been raining hard this month. At night, the concrete walls of the house amplify the ominous rumblings of thunder that reverberate across the night sky, making it hard to sleep.

But each morning, Vicentas—ancient, bronze and bow-legged—launches herself up those concrete stairs, mop in hand, zeroing in on the puddle of water that, even now, is slowly expanding, drop by drop on the landing.

It's the same puddle that was there a week ago, a month ago, two years ago.

Short of breath and clammy with sweat, she does not stop to rest or pause. The way she swings that mop and climbs those steps—it fills you with a certain dread just to watch her. But you cannot help but watch her. She sweeps and dusts with such savage intensity, you feel a little feeble yourself, just sitting there with your hot tea, trying to look occupied and important.

By now, you would think a woman of that incalculable age would have somehow resolved her argument with the world. But I suppose the dirt and grime that blows in from off the dusty street are ample grist for her mill—or perhaps there's something else.

Last night, just as we were about to turn in, I saw that scorpion again, halfway up the wall above the staircase, too high to be hit with a broom, but not so high that you would take no notice.

I've seen Vicentas take an angry swipe at it with her mop and nearly lose her balance, cursing and muttering all the while in words I could neither decipher nor comprehend. And it was there again yesterday, looking even more menacing than usual, the tip of its stinger flexed and threatening.

This morning as usual, Vicentas was making her advance upon the house with her brigade of buckets and brooms. She came bustling past, not paying me the slightest notice, her threadbare slippers shuffling and scraping on the cool concrete floor—and her old, swollen fingers in a death-grip around the mop handle.

Barely able to catch her breath and unwilling to rest for even a moment, she's up those stairs in a flash, her dark eyes locked on her antagonist: that revolting insect that she will eradicate once and for all, and maybe get some peace from all these well-fed gringos and screeching parrots and barking dogs and clanging church bells at the break of dawn, and those screaming boys next door with nothing but sticks and bottle-tops to play with.

And so she swings that wet mop-head over her shoulder and swipes with enough force to wipe every living thing from off the face of this rundown, ramshackle world—but misses the wall completely.

It is simply another moment or two of cosmic inevitability that draws the wet and weighty mop past her shoulder, bending her wrists to a breaking point, so that she arches backwards, loses her balance, and falls like the tail of a meteor, as first the mop-head and then her thin, bony Aztec frame go airborne off the staircase, landing headfirst on the concrete floor with a dull, splintering thud.

She does not stir again.

I observed all this from over the pages of a paperback novel I was reading. The house was momentarily silent, and I thought how pleasant and surprising the sound of that silence really was.

Then the parrot on the roof started shrieking, the dog in the next garden resumed its pointless barking, and the water in the kettle reached a whistling boil.

If by Postcard

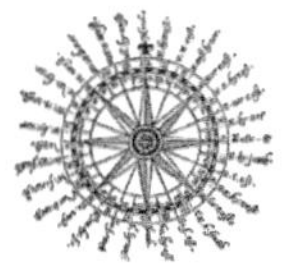

SOMETIMES break-ups arrive by letter—sometimes by postcard; of the two, I by far prefer the letter.

I wouldn't want to create the impression that men are always leaving me, I've left a few myself, yet I must confess that Eric was a surprise.

With his composer's intensity, expressive hands, and long ponytail, he had made me feel—while perhaps not young again—at least that possibility might lift me once more upon its wings.

We had first met in a voice class that I was teaching. A friend of his had persuaded him that voice lessons might help him with his latest composition—a symphonic movement with choral interludes.

Tall, boyishly handsome, and shy—I guess that about describes my weakness in men. Eric was all of these. He had stuttered as a child but now, in his mid-thirties, it was only infrequently that he did so—whenever he became overly self-conscious.

"Er-er-eric Walker....I write mu-music," he had said, when I had asked everyone in the class to introduce themselves.

I myself was one year into a blissful divorce from Frank, my first husband. And while I had dated a little, being with Eric was like marching to the beat of a new drum.

"Breathing from the diaphragm..." I had said, as I placed a flattened palm against his belly to demonstrate the point. He had gulped a deep breath in surprise.

Later on after class, we went out for drinks. I ended up telling him my war stories from the marriage, and he told me about his sister, Janice, a woman my age who was about to get divorced and was planning a move to Mexico.

That got us talking about murals and mariachis, and when we ended up that night at my place, the affair, you might say, was on.

Still, looking back, I will admit that being with a younger man was a little like knowing that someday, somehow, someone was going to call in the loan—but for the time being, you could string things along with nothing more than bright smiles and minimum payments.

It had been a long time since I'd opened up this much to anyone, and truthfully, I luxuriated in the almost reckless, headlong dive into desire.

Then, one evening, feeling dangerously romantic and lighter in spirit than I had for a long time, I wagered those three little words that seem to heave so much weight—and just like that, the angels fled. Suddenly, the full-throated choir we were in went a cappella—and it was only me alone on the stage, my voice hoarse and thin; the glare of the spotlight pinning me in place.

When he stopped inviting me out with his other musician friends, I knew we were in trouble. And though I may have been the wiser of the two, I was surprised at the depth of my disappointment.

Then it was July, and I was off to Venice to teach a semester overseas. Eric had planned to join me at the end of the month and we were going to "do" Italy, but there never was a second act.

Break-ups, when they arrive by letter, give you something to return to, like an artifact of yourself, still cared for and preserved in the delicate folds of a faded envelope.

Those who write letters seem to be grappling with the forces in life that push and pull and somehow drag you, unwillingly, towards your destiny. They make their protestations, they even doubt their choices, but in the end, they tell you that for good or bad, for better or worse, it has to be this way—that they simply must move on.

Postcard writers, on the other hand, like my Eric, have already moved on.

They are moving at full speed away from the white-hot center of their emotions and have found just a quick moment to say they are sorry, that it was great while it lasted, but "goodbye" anyway.

If by postcard, break-ups arrive like news flashes — living only in the fragile space between today's headlines and yesterday's news.

Of the two, I will always prefer the letter.

Sour Times

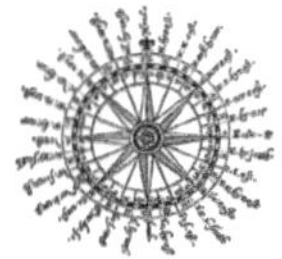

GORDON was ecstatic to see us once again, even though we had met just once before—during our first-ever visit to that expatriate Mexican town.

We were introduced at a local art gallery, a popular gathering spot for expats. Gordon had been waiting on his date, but she had evidently stood him up. Being in his mid-60s, handsome, and comfortably retired, he had enough self-worth in reserve to "let it slide," as he had said with a shrug.

Now, a year later, Elsie and I were back in Mexico on sabbatical, and when Gordon spotted us at the local cantina, he greeted us with wide-open arms, as though we were his long lost children.

Beaming, he insisted that we dine with him at his new hacienda, up in the foothills above the town.

Since we didn't have a car, he offered to return later in the evening to pick us up. And so just after sunset, we found ourselves settled into the leather seats of a silver

Mercedes, winding up through the dusty, cobblestone roads that led to his gated property.

Elsie and I had grown quite used to playing the part of other people's children. As students, we had scratched our way through college, and after we graduated, we decided to settle in Berkeley, California, most often finding ourselves among other people's families during holidays.

We possessed enough charm and intelligence to add color to almost any gathering. While most people had a woven fabric of familial bonds and memories, we had a mosaic—a couple of years with this family, another with the next—moving in and out of context as circumstances dictated. So once we had settled into Gordon's hillside homestead, we had a pretty good sense of how things were going to play out.

Gordon and his wife were separated. She lived in Canada. He paid her bills, helped run her small business, and exchanged notes with her over the fax machine once or twice a month.

We learned he had a grown son and daughter, too, though he hadn't seen either of them in more than a year. He was particularly bitter about his son who, he said, was too busy trying to save the planet than find time to call his own father.

"Fucking liberal bastards," he sneered, as he attempted to describe the crowd his son hung out with, never pausing to consider that Elsie and I were both Liberal Arts graduates ourselves.

Elsie headed over to Gordon's recliner and draped her

long legs over one of the armrests. I sat on a stool at his marble kitchen counter, sipping expensive, single-malt scotch, listening to stories of how he had bought and sold one business after the other.

Elsie flipped aimlessly through the pages of a magazine. She soon grew restless and began strolling around the living room, inspecting knick-knacks on Gordon's shelves and peeking behind cupboard doors. It was what any daughter would do who'd been away from home for a while.

I was beginning to tire of Gordon's boorishness myself, and his mood was growing darker the more he drank. We had some steaks marinating in the fridge, but no one made the slightest gesture towards starting the grill.

It finally occurred to Gordon to ask me what I did for a living, and the more details I provided about being an untenured, assistant professor of Comparative Literature, the more I could sense his growing disdain. He was beginning to eye Elsie, too, glancing over at her with growing irritation.

Then, from the corner of my eye, I saw Elsie reach out and slip something from one of Gordon's shelves into her purse.

The sudden rat-a-tat-tat of a fax machine filled the room. Gordon wiped his mouth and swung off his stool to see what was up. It was sad in a way, knowing that rather than a letter or spontaneous love note from a sweetheart, it was most likely another communiqué from his ex-wife, asking when she could expect the next check to help prop up the new boutique soap company she was trying to jump-start in Vancouver.

Elsie shot a glance over at me and tilted her head towards the door. I took her cue, and while Gordon fussed over the fax machine, I grabbed one of the expensive bottles of Cabernet he had bought for our little family reunion and stuffed it into my backpack.

"Gordon," I called out, "Elsie's not feeling great, we're gonna take off."

Gordon looked back over his shoulder. I picked up his car keys and dangled them in the air. "Can I borrow your car to take her home? I'll bring it back later tonight."

Gordon simply nodded his head and waved a dismissive hand at me. Sons always ask their fathers to borrow the car—it's the most natural thing in the world.

I clutched the keys in my hand and we headed out. We climbed into Gordon's Mercedes, turned the ignition, and the engine roared to life.

"Where d'ya wanna head?" I asked Elsie.

"Let's drive out to the country," she said, 'I hear there's a meteor shower tonight."

I pulled a U-turn and gunned the engine. The wheels spun for a moment on the gravel driveway, and then we were gone.

I knew dad didn't mind. He was used to eating alone.

The Hidden World

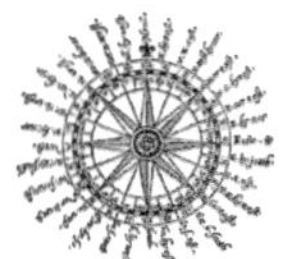

I BELIEVE there's a hidden world that, on this particular April morning, walking in the park, hearing the surf crash against the rocks, with the wind blowing through the Cyprus trees and the sky intentionally blue and flawless—reveals itself to be something highly selective and not at all obvious to the casual observer.

Sometimes this sensation, alive with desire, will only be heightened by the introduction of a beautiful young girl with cherry-red toenails and a pair of white-rimmed sunglasses that, together with the ability of shrubs to suddenly burst into clusters of purple flowers, produces something like joy, which is also a key with which to enter this hidden world.

Then my sweet Antoinette will send a text message, asking when we can meet. And I will have to tell her that my car has broken down again and there is nothing I can do now to change that.

Then her lips will curl into a pout and she will not

be happy to hear this. She'll stop sending messages and will later on accuse me of taking her for granted, which is exactly how the sky and trees are not being treated, or so she'll say.

And this will be the beginning of a dark exchange that will move in over us like a gray cloud; until once again, hours later, the hidden world will call out from a golden poppy in a language that only a lover could fathom.

And so a balance will finally be achieved. I will tell Antoinette that if she can just wait until morning, I will arrive at her door with warm rolls, fresh coffee, and a smile she can store in her heart for as long as she needs.

And then she will say that this is her lucky day, her happy day; and she, too, will see an opening to the hidden world—one that was planted in her heart, a long time ago.

Before I Go

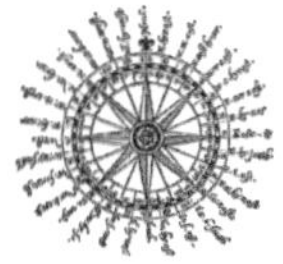

I'M NOT a huge fan of commercial air travel. The lines seem longer, the seats smaller, and the legroom narrower. Or maybe I'm just getting older.

It's not easy to admit, but I'm growing more accustomed to the kindly, sympathetic looks I get now from the young women who, to my own eyes, still look entirely desirable. More fool me, I suppose.

I'm huddled in this cramped plane for one reason only—my mother is dying, and I'm doing what any decent son would do—be there for her final hours, bury her, and preside at her funeral.

She and I were never close. She always preferred her musical protégés over her own son, who couldn't string two notes of music together even if my life depended on it.

Seated beside me is a young man in his twenties. He says nothing but stares intently at a three-inch-wide screen, punching tiny keys with his thumbs in response to the flailing arms and legs of some miniature gladiator game.

I wonder about a generation so steeped in the figures of synthetic, make-believe worlds that are painless, transitory, and one-dimensional. Perhaps they'll live lives less rich in feeling. Or maybe they'll just be more pragmatic, less inclined to brood on existential worries and more capable of seeing death and mortality for what it is, and to not think a moment more about it.

I myself am at an age where, more often than not, the present is simply the space where I second-guess the past. I feel like the last man standing on a small island that is gradually receding as the tides slowly erase the landscape that I once recognized as my life.

Outside the window and far below, I can see the snow-capped peaks of the Rocky Mountains as the plane drones on towards New York.

I daydream about what it would be like if we just went down. You hand over your life whenever you walk on board a plane.

I often try to imagine what it feels like to die. All I know is that before I go, I'd like to watch the first stars appearing against a wide, indigo sky. I'd like to stand at the edge of the ocean at sunset and feel the evening winds blowing in my face as the sky spills molten gold and purple across the horizon.

Before I go, I'd like to look this world squarely in the eye and say, "This is the world I have known. These are the people who I have loved and who have traveled with me through this thin slice of time. We will not come this way again."

Before I go, I'd like to cup this handful of consolation in my hands and, drawing in my last breath, breathe out '*Yes*' to whoever may be listening.

32

The Odds

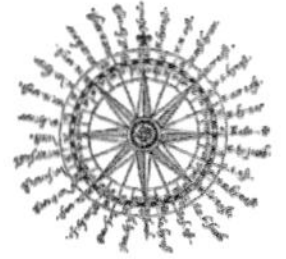

BLIND FAITH—what is that anyway? I'm a believer in probabilities and odds, which I suppose makes perfect sense for an incurable gambler like me.

If the odds look good, then count me in. But if I've got to pray for it—well, somehow I just don't get that same warm, fuzzy feeling inside.

Connie, my wife, she's a different story altogether. She's got a prayer for everything: a safe flight, a good meal, missing kids—there are very few things in her world that aren't worth praying for.

She'll often say, *'There's no harm in being specific, darlin', the good Lord hears them all, so you may as well lay it on the line.'*

I can't fault her there. Naturally, she's not too keen on the card playing—or the drinking, either. And I don't mind saying, I've had a few tonight, which is why I'm out in the shed, making like I'm fixing that old rocking chair I'm always promising to put right.

We bought that chair when she was pregnant with

our son, Evan. It's funny how time passes. When that boy was weaned, this old rocker ended up on the front porch where, over the years, the elements slowly took their toll. It's a beauty, though, built by the Amish community over in West Virginia. My cousin Gerald trucked it all the way here for us.

Of course, Evan's a young man now. He's at a small arts college in Austin, Texas. It's been about two weeks now, since the accident. He was out late, carousing at the football stadium, which of course was supposed to be closed and off-limits that time of night. They say he fell from the bleachers and got a pretty good crack on the head. He's been in a coma since then.

I hear the odds are about three-to-one of someone coming out of a coma within the first two weeks. After that, the odds start dropping proportionately. I'm putting my money on those three-to-one odds, since I know I won't get a better deal than that, no matter how you cut it.

And prayer? Well, I'd be lying if I told you I weren't doing some of that myself tonight. I'm laying a big wager that there's a God up there in heaven—a beautiful and compassionate God who will hear our prayers and who will bring our Evan back to us, from wherever it is he's gone.

Truth is, I hope there's a God listening to all the prayers that are rising up tonight—in this town, the next town, and across this whole country—a sky wide with prayer, filling God's ear with the music of all us lost souls.

Before & After

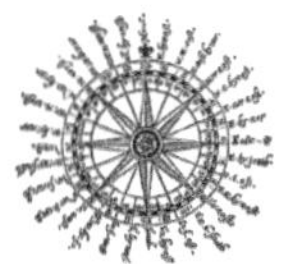

THE FULL-COLOR feature article lays open in front of us, casting a spell that no one at the table can resist.

My new, hip friends who invite me now to their dinner parties insist that I bring along copies of the magazine. They open the spread and show off the dazzling photos that unveil the hidden lives of those they envy, or secretly despise.

They admire the artful layout, the interplay of words and images, and even the letters beneath the headlines that spell out my name.

Before, I was just one skinny twenty-something among millions. Now, after the magazine articles, I am Nina W., insider to the unspeakably rich of Europe and the Middle East; the one who, like the spoiled, wealthy kids I shadowed last summer, slept all day and partied all night in the members-only nightclubs of Bali, Singapore, and Malaysia.

The exposé stirs interest and garners attention, but the magical ingredient is me. The story is simply the spell, but I am the sorceress, in person, the one who made the journey and then returned, before and after—first ignored, last desired.

Before, I was no one's flower: boys found me boring, and the girls couldn't get past the wonder of their own selves; experimental, pliable, barometric.

Now, I've become something else—a force, a desire, a drive that dresses up in costume—a player who others want to be near, to seduce, to own, to borrow, to discover, to solve—to do everything with except see with clear eyes what is alive and dark and awakened within me.

They are all honed in on me now, as they usually are, even the married ones. What they see is something they misinterpret as hunger, curiosity, or vulnerability. What they cannot see is this deep emptiness that would swallow each and every one of them. It is a darkness that has grown within me like a seed these past few months, a winter that promises only a paper spring, a fragrant blossom that offers a secret perfume of nothingness.

For those gathered at this table, I stand apart and alone, as I suppose one would, if this before is to have no after, other than the one that will live on in their minds the next time they gather to eat, to talk, or to remember me.

Tomorrow—the World

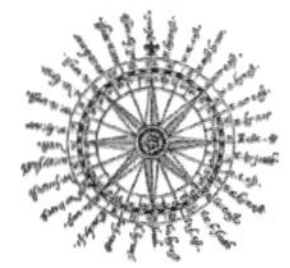

I'M UP, Vic, are you?

Reggie's asleep in the next room, and I'm sitting here in the kitchen thinking about you—and thinking about us.

There are so many things I like about you, Vic—your warmth, your kindness, and your sense of humor. I guess that's why I agreed to that first date with you—I needed someone to bring some laughter into my life, and you always knew how to make me laugh.

But I can't do this anymore, Vic.

Trish asked me today why I can't pick her up on Thursdays, after ballet. It's one thing to be cheating on your husband, but it's another to be cheating on your child. And I can't keep living in two worlds. What I need is one world where everything within it is whole and complete.

I'm not interested in pressuring you, Vic, that's the last thing I'd want to do. But you can't cheat on yourself—you understand that, don't you? You can't be only half yourself with me and half yourself with your wife—that's not what living is all about.

I know this will sound strange, but I've been thinking a lot about grace lately, and what it means. I think grace is about bringing out all the richness that's within us. I think the more honest we are about becoming our true selves, the closer we get to God. At least that's how I see it tonight, Vic.

Tomorrow, everything changes. First, I'm going to ask Reggie for a divorce. Then I'm going to make good on a few promises I've made to myself.

I'm going to head across the country to Utah to see my sister Michelle and her new baby girl. Next, I'm going down to Texas to be with my friend, Connie, whose poor son is in hospital in a coma.

Then, I'm going to follow my dream, Vic, and drive across the border to that small town in Mexico I've been telling you about. I'm bringing Trish, too, and we're going to start all over again, with or without you.

We're going to point the car in the direction of our dreams—to a place where I know our true selves will be waiting; a place where it's warm and the nights are long and where we'll wear silver bracelets on our wrists and cotton shawls around our shoulders, where they play music in the streets at night, and where you can wear sandals all year round, even in winter.

Tonight, it's just you and me Vic, but tomorrow—the world.

Brainpower

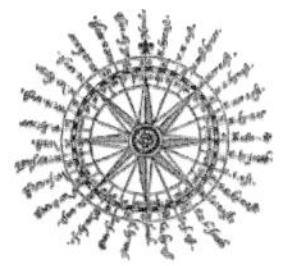

LAST WEEK, I read a newspaper article saying that the polar ice caps are melting. Sea levels, they say, are rising. Most of the glaciers are beginning to melt, too.

I saw a photograph recently that caught a huge shelf of ice splintering and slipping into the ocean—a floating ice-cube about the size of Manhattan.

But grappling with the causes of global warming is not for everyone—I understand that. Most people are occupied simply trying to figure out what it is they'll have for dinner tonight.

This, I'm certain, is mainly on account of the fact that the brain is really only a highly functioning filter, engineered not so much to apprehend the world, as many of us have been taught, but to actually limit the huge amount of stimuli that, if left unchecked, would bury us in a virtual avalanche of information.

Consider death, for instance. Mortality and certain

death are perfect examples of the kinds of unprofitable stimuli that, on a daily basis, the brain excels at filtering out. And a good thing too. Who needs a daily reminder that we're inching closer to death each passing day? Not me, at least.

Global warming, rising sea levels, the shrinking ozone: it's all fairly extraneous to the day-to-day machinations of the standard-issue brain.

The brain, under the influence of highly persuasive biological motivators, is strictly programmed to orchestrate and engineer procreation which, from the standpoint of the average Homo Sapiens, is what you call a win-win situation.

Except, of course, for overpopulation, reports and ample evidence of which, the brain is more than adept at filtering out. Global consequences in general register nary a blip on the average, oscillating brain wave.

There are those, however, who on the surface appear truly dedicated to planetary issues. But upon closer examination, we may discover that it is sex, rather than good global citizenship, that is at root of these drives.

How so? Those brains understand that strongly shared communal values, such as the kind derived from environmental concerns, are often quite conducive to mediating relations with the opposite sex.

And so again, the drive for procreation rears its ugly head, even if you're thinking globally, not locally.

Me? Well, I just read the headlines and call them as I see 'em. I've lived so long in New York City, I honestly believe Columbus Avenue is the center of the earth.

How do I know this? I was riding the bus last week when the actor Bob Newhart hopped on board and took a seat right behind me. Evolutionary consciousness being what it is, I turned to him and nodded. He looked warily at me and returned to gazing out the window. Most of what goes on in the world happens when you're looking out the window, so I didn't fault him a bit.

I saw another report recently about a famous glacier that calved just outside of Juneau, Alaska. Some guy kayaking nearby tipped over and froze to death in the icy water within a matter of minutes.

But it was unbearably hot that day on Columbus Avenue, and there were many cars all trying to advance in front of one another. Bob Newhart maintained a calm, steady gaze out the window. Most of the other brains in midtown Manhattan were calculating their lunch options.

I, too, was calculating my options, but my brain felt like a stone lodged against the glass wall of my skull. I remained in my seat and sat quietly until we reached the end of the line. I waited for the driver to switch the destination sign, and then I traveled back along the route—the same way I had come.

42

Tonight, You Can See Jupiter

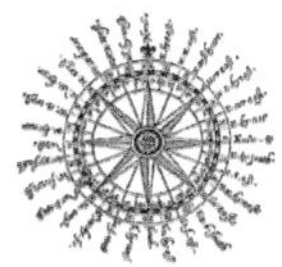

THESE DAYS, I'm playing the arterial version of Russian roulette, indulging in the comfort of high-fat double lattes and glazed doughnuts. And although it may be wrong; I know it is *right*.

I mean it is right in the sense that I can accept with absolute certainty that my body desires and craves these things. Such assurances are worth their weight in gold these days.

The town I live in has no particular distinction, other than it's a suburb, spun out from the flash-point of a city that was once surrounded by vast sand dunes, designated on maps by the earliest 19th century city planners as "uninhabitable."

Well, here we all are—just try finding a parking spot on a Saturday afternoon.

I suppose that's the thing about destiny, it happens with or without our consent. Only the fixed stars remain constant. With them, you could navigate anywhere, if you knew where it was you were going.

There's a part of me living life through the wrong end of the telescope these days. The millions of stars in the night sky are only other people's choices. My options have been narrowed.

Annabel is the love of my life right now. She's also my landlord. I live in the in-law apartment she and her ex-husband built in sunnier times. He's in Reno now, with some younger version of the girl of his dreams, while Annabel got the real estate.

The in-law is not a bad place; just a little makeshift. Annabel's washer and dryer butt up against the wall of my living room, and on wash days, the spin cycle will nearly shake the pictures off the wall. Lately though, I've been spending nights upstairs with her.

I guess the thing that got me started on Annabel was her name. I had asked her whether her father or someone in the family had a thing for Edgar Allen Poe. She said her Dad wasn't a big reader, and didn't Edgar Allan Poe write *Frankenstein*...?

It was no matter. Annabel takes me by the hand and leads me through the park. She points out the names of plants as we pass them by. If she didn't have me to haul around, she'd have to get a dog. Annabel needs to lead, and I'm the perfect foil. With nothing but unfinished novels and a laundry list of part-time jobs, my trail-blazing days are fading fast behind me.

I'm not sure this is right—my tenuous relationship

with a separated, not-quite-divorced older woman. Am I searching for absolutes? I suppose I am.

It feels like I've been waging a battle of will against destiny, searching for that one fixed point upon which my entire being would be centered.

And that's the thing about the narrator in Annabel Lee—he wasn't going to let a little thing like death stand in the way of his desire. He had located the one fixed compass point of his reality, and he was hanging with it clear through to the other side of sanity.

I'm not cut from that mold. And besides, Annabel would slap me up the side of the head if I ever started in about loving her beyond life or any such nonsense.

Nope. There's something to be said for letting go in the heat of a struggle. You can pull and push and prod only so far, until you reach a point where suddenly, you lose sight of what it is you were battling for.

Then, all you have left is the battle—the struggle. The purpose has been left behind in some outdated idea of what it was all supposed to mean or add up to.

I've been thinking about this all night now, and I've been waiting for Annabel to join me outside so I can show her the stars.

It's a cool, spring evening; not warm enough yet to stand out here without a hat or coat, but crisp and very clear—yes, very clear.

I know I might sound foolish for saying this, but tonight, you can see Jupiter.

46

Night Vigil

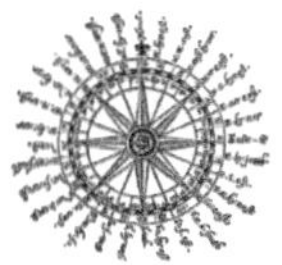

I HAVE come to sit beside Mrs. Riesman while she dies. It is late, and her house is still; her night-nurse will be here soon.

Mrs. Riesman was my piano teacher and my first mentor. She always saw the best in me. She somehow knew how to support my own dimly formed ideas about who or what I might become when I grew up.

I learned almost everything I know about concert music listening to Mrs. Riesman's record collection. Growing up, my parents and I would spend most Sunday afternoons at the Riesman's apartment down the hall. Mr. Riesman and my father would play chess, while Mrs. Riesman presided over her beloved record player, filling the apartment with the sounds of Mozart, Brahms, and Bach.

Whenever she and I were alone together, as we were for most piano lessons, Mrs. Riesman would try to coach me about my stuttering—a subject that was strictly taboo in my own household.

"Eric," she'd say, rolling the 'r' in her Eastern European accent, "take a deep breath; in, out—take your time, not rush."

Soon after my thirteenth birthday, I remember her telling me that only really intelligent people stuttered. It was immeasurably reassuring to hear someone say that, especially another adult.

Mr. and Mrs. Riesman faithfully attended every local recital I gave. I always made sure they had seats up front.

Years later, long after she had taught me everything she could about the piano, Mrs. Riesman liked to tease me about why it was I hadn't settled down and married. Frankly, I still wonder about that myself.

Perhaps I'm clinging to the idea that only after I've written every piano concerto I'm ever going to write; only after I've mastered every sonata I want to play—then, and only then, will I be worthy of someone's life-long love and commitment.

I like to think that I'm old and wise enough now to recognize the obvious flaws in my own reasoning, but I'm about to do it again—back out of another perfectly viable relationship.

Yet how could I even begin to explain all this to another person? For one thing, I'd be stuttering from the outset, and then it would only get worse as the person would inevitably try to encourage me to relax and pull my words together.

My words—I swear they arrive as if spilling from a

waterfall, linking together a constellation of connections and meanings. But, for whatever reason, the moment I actually start to speak them, they careen into each other and go skidding off my tongue, so that I'm chasing after them, trying to fit them into place—the way I know in my mind they must go.

And perhaps for that reason alone, I think it would be best to write a letter, or better yet, a postcard. I could explain in a few well-chosen lines what it would take me an eternity to express over drinks or dinner.

Mrs. Riesman is breathing quietly now. Her once long, red hair has all turned gray. An antique, silver hairbrush rests on her bedside table, and I pick it up and pull it across a lock of hair that has fallen across her forehead.

She's navigating her final departure to wherever it is we all must go, and she is going it alone from here on out.

I notice her eyes moving beneath her eyelids. Every so often, she draws her right hand to her mouth and her fingertips lightly touch her lower lip. She is utterly unaware of doing this, but watching her, I can imagine her reviewing scenes from her life, considering each vignette as it floats into view—then letting it go forever.

"It's okay," I whisper, as I gently pull the brush across another lock of fine, silver hair, "it'll be alright."

And I really don't know whether I'm saying this to her, or whether I'm saying it to myself.

I suppose in the big picture, it doesn't really matter.

Letter to Evie

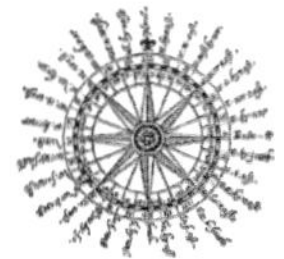

I HOPE you don't mind me writing out of the blue like this, but at our age, I think it's nice to reconnect with old friends—at least I hope it is.

I bet winter is really shaping up there in Montréal! I remember how you always hated the winters, so I can only imagine how troubled your old bones are now, living in such a cold and unforgiving climate.

I finally moved down to Florida with Etta, Judy, and Earl. The four of us make a small, strange tribe, but we don't mind. Etta and Judy even started yoga this year. Earl still chain-smokes; and me, well, I'm a little unsteady on my feet these days—but I still manage.

I've been having the strangest dreams lately. Last night, I dreamed I was stuck at the top of a ladder, trying to enter my house through an open window. I was afraid the ladder would slip out from underneath and leave me dangling from the ledge, hanging on for dear life.

I don't have a clue what that dream was about, but

when I awoke this morning, I thought it was time I unpacked some of that old baggage from the past and dropped you a line.

I've been thinking a lot about the old days, though you probably wouldn't expect that—you and me jagging here and there in that old Mustang my dad bought me.

Do you remember that one evening we had parked across the street from the local baseball diamond? The sun was setting and everything was growing still—just the green symmetry of that field, the sky on fire with orange— and you and me sitting there staring out through the windshield, like we were watching the second-coming.

Then Paul ambled up to the car, tapped on the window, and asked if he could bum a cigarette. I know it's ancient history now—who stole whose boyfriend—but the rift between us never quite healed, did it dear?

I didn't know much about anything back then, much less anything about love. But I do know that eventually we both found our way—you and Brian, and me and Paul. I did receive your card by the way, after Paul's passing, so thanks for that.

It's strange when you lose a mate; even though they're gone, something of their presence stays behind, attaching itself to you like a weightless reminder of the times you had and the places you went.

Sometimes I sense your presence, too, walking next to me, though I know you hate the Florida heat and the white-shorts-and-tennis crowd.

Anyhow, I am alone now, but not without company.

Etta should be here shortly, and so will Earl, if he ever wakes up from his nap, which at our age is always a toss-up.

Give my fond regards to Montréal. If you ever decide to trade in the hats and coats and get with the hedonists, you know where to find us.

Paul always cared deeply for you, too, you know. He told me so not very long ago, just as things really started to go downhill.

I believe that love affairs, once they're over, live on in the shadows we cast each day—when we're out in the sun, or looking out at the sea, or simply shutting our eyes for the briefest of moments to remember the ones we loved, as they pass through our thoughts as soft as a whisper; as intimate as a sigh.

54

Floating in the Gray

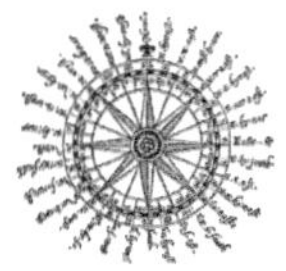

THE LAST TIME I saw Dale, we shook hands and parted, after having just returned from our yearly ritual of traversing the Golden Gate Bridge.

It was a commitment we had honored every November for nearly fifteen years, rain or shine. We'd talk about our lives, our marriages, our jobs, our hopes, and our disappointments. It was a gentleman's agreement. No small talk, no false bravado, just two kindred souls laying it on the line.

On our last walk, Dale was in a particularly dark frame of mind. His small business had been on the ropes for some time, but the last economic downturn had delivered the knockout punch. His house was in foreclosure, his wife wanted out, and he told me that all in all, he was ready to reinvent himself.

I felt a little sorry for him, I'll admit; but I was equally intrigued by his notion of reinvention—it was a preoccupation of my own. Almost everywhere I've ever visited, I've considered re-making my life there. Other people's lives always seem more interesting and fulfilling than my own.

On the way back across the bridge, I told Dale about my recent trip to the East Coast to bury my mother. I told him how I felt my own world was shrinking. I said I just couldn't imagine living to be an age where I needed a nurse or some stranger to change my underwear. I just wouldn't let that happen—I'd rather be dead.

I described to him how I'd met one of my mother's musical protégés at the funeral and how he had stuttered when he tried to tell me how much he had appreciated all my mother's support and encouragement. We ended up exchanging a few laughs over our women troubles—one topic, at least, to which we could both relate.

As Dale and I reached the mid-point of the bridge, a sudden gust of wind buffeted us, and Dale's baseball cap sailed off his head and flipped over the railing. We perched over the guardrail like two kids, looking down into the churning dark green water below. It occurred to us then just how easy it would be to launch oneself over the side and drop into oblivion.

They say that hitting the water from the height of the bridge is like landing on concrete; very few who've jumped ever survive. You have to hit feet-first to even stand a chance. I told Dale that if I were to jump, I'd make sure I fell face up, looking up towards the sky while I dropped backwards into eternity.

Together, we stared down at the water and out across

the bay, towards Angel Island and Alcatraz. Sailing boats dotted the landscape, though moment by moment, the fog was making it hard to see anything at all.

"I've always been curious why so many people choose to jump from this bridge," Dale said, still staring down at the water.

"Me, too," I replied.

The fog was thick and heavy by now, and a wet wind stung our faces. And then we were nowhere—just formless beings suspended in a dense, damp cloud. There was no landscape, no structure, only the constant pressure of wet air pummeling our bodies, soaking our clothes, and reducing our visibility to zero.

"I've actually decided to make a move and leave here for a while," Dale said, turning towards me. "Next week, I'm heading up to the high desert to see if maybe I can get a new perspective on things."

It was still dreary and gray by the time we made it back to the parking lot. We shook hands, and Dale got into his car and drove away.

My first thought was to get home and change into some dry clothes. But then I had a different impulse—one that had been incubating within me for some time now. And so I turned around, and facing a damp November wind, I took my first, slow steps back across the span.

Love is Blind

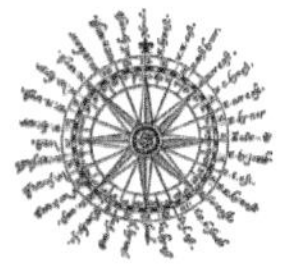

I WAS BORN incomplete—stricken with a congenital defect that would leave me blind by the time I turned five.

But there had been that certain moment, before darkness fully drowned me, when I had glimpsed the image of what I can only describe as perfection. It was a woman's face, gazing down at me in my infant's crib.

I can still trace her outline in the haunted air with my fingertips. I can still conjure those dark, deep-set eyes and her long, black hair falling over her shoulders. Like an after-image burned into my brain, that icon of feminine beauty has remained alive within me—seeking its own completion.

As I inched forward through the years, feeling my way along the stone walls of this dusty town, tapping out the steps to the curb's edge, a part of me has remained alert, always waiting for the sound of a voice that I knew someday would save me.

With the same faith that I placed in the punctual rising of the morning sun, I knew that somehow I would find her, or that she would find me—and I would transform this loneliness that has clung to me for as long as I can remember.

And then, one cold December morning, huddled at the curb, waiting for the lights to change, I heard a voice offer me an arm. It was a voice full of self-assurance and concern.

I lifted my elbow and she took hold with a firm, confident grip. This was my Marie-José. She has been my companion now for nearly three years. And though she herself is not perfect, her imperfections exist only in the temporal world, far from the place where ideals inhabit.

She, too, has had her crosses to bear, but those scars that line her neck are nothing more to me than assurances that she is real, that she has lived, and that she, too, has persevered, despite heartbreaks and misfortune.

And those church bells that toll so faithfully each morning, they remind me of what it is I have come to understand after all these years—that only others can complete us—that no matter how deeply personal our own incompleteness, we cannot give to ourselves that which only others can offer to us.

But what is it that I can offer to Marie-José in return?

Only this—to listen as only the sightless can listen. To hear without prejudice or distraction, letting the sounds of her voice rise and fall within me, without judgment, without amendment, without self-interest.

In the deep well of my listening, Marie-José finds her completion.

62

Gold Digger

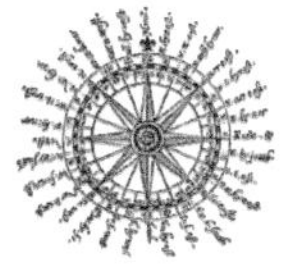

I HAVE BEEN digging since dawn this morning, and no matter how hard I try to reason myself out of it, I cannot stop digging. But it is not the mound of dirt or pile of pitchforks and shovels that disturbs me most—it's the neighbors.

One of them, I'm certain, has just finished dialing the police. The other is watching me from behind her drapes, and although she is partially concealed, I can detect with no lack of certainty, the posture of revulsion and contempt.

It all began yesterday afternoon while I was pacing the front lawn, sweeping my hand-held metal detector just inches above the ground. Suddenly the needle on the meter swung to indicate precious metal. "Gold!" I told myself—that, or certainly some priceless artifact from antiquity.

I grabbed a small hand shovel and started to dig, but after an hour, I came up empty—all I had was a hole large enough to plant a small tree.

So, I dug harder and faster. Beads of sweat dripped from my forehead and ran into my eyes and stung. It wasn't much longer before I came to the conclusion that what the situation really called for was machinery.

I tossed down my gloves and headed over to the local home-improvement center. I slapped down my deposit on a 25-horsepower, single-seat backhoe—'Ideal for the Do-It-Yourself Landscaper,' the sign had read.

I hitched the vehicle up to the rear of my car and drove home. I pulled up in front, straddled the seat, and fired up the engine. It rumbled to life, burping a plume of thick, black smoke into the air.

I kicked it into gear and rode up the sidewalk, crushing a line of border hedges along the way. Soon I was excavating at a rate of four feet a minute. I knew that if I just kept digging, the pay-off would surely be worth it.

I am now standing at the edge of a precipice twelve feet wide and twenty feet deep, and frankly, I'm a little concerned.

I'll be the first to admit that I may have reached the edge of that proverbial limb. But for me, to stop digging is to admit that your neighbors are right; that you are a middle-aged lunatic who has finally flipped his lid, just as they had always suspected. To stop digging is to believe what your sixth-grade math teacher said about you. To stop digging is to admit that you no longer possess the will to conquer your heart's desires, no matter how quixotic.

To stop digging is to give in to every murmur of self-doubt that you have ever had—to acquiesce to the weakling in you who simply wants to pick up his marbles and go home.

To stop digging is to confess to the one god above that you are not worthy—that you are of no more consequence than a tattered moth, hopelessly circling an amber porch light. To stop digging is to drown your dreams like unwanted kittens in the nearest river.

But beyond all that, to stop digging is to surrender. And on this hot summer afternoon, with the warm sun slowly sinking towards the horizon and the air vibrating with the sounds of insects and birdsong, there is—and will be—no surrender.

When it Comes Time

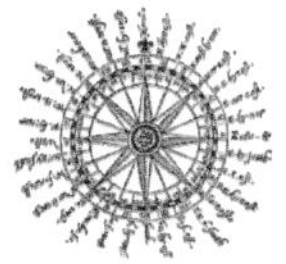

WHEN IT COMES time for me to take a man, I will divest myself of all my masks, free myself from all my compulsions, and in one stroke, extinguish the constellations of chaos that orbit above me. Only then will I begin to clear a path that leads to me, so that my man, whoever he may be, will see me standing in the clearing and find himself a foothold.

And he will surely need a foothold to anchor himself against the mountain of newspapers that I've been collecting since the 1980s, the heaps of vintage clothes that have burst beyond the confines of my closet, and the plants—they're in the sink and in the bathtub, they're on ledges and on countertops.

I suppose I am not the type to easily yield.

There are boxes of garage-sale acquisitions that have never been inventoried, and never will be. There are at least three cats, and perhaps a couple more that appear now and then for dinner. There is room for everything in my apartment except for one thing—a man.

But since my mother's passing, I've slowly been able to set things aside and let go a little. To my amazement, I actually tossed out a three-foot pile of old National Geographic magazines last week. It may sound selfish, but now that she's gone, there's a scent of freedom in the air. All my protections have been suddenly rendered obsolete.

There were no tears, either—just the news that arrived by registered mail from her lawyers, followed by the silence of the morning.

When the day comes for me to take a man, I will simply leave behind the cluttered confines of my daily routines, without comment. I will set aside all my encumbrances and, like one who lays down her weapons, I will embrace all that is before me with the simple tools of my eyes, my ears, and my limbs.

On that day, I will give myself away.

After You

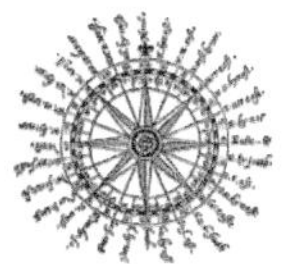

ELI WAS, by any measure, an exemplar of gentlemanly manners. He had recently befriended my wife's best friend Carol—and up until the time he crashed his black Land Rover through the front window of the local Rite-Aid pharmacy—he had never done anything out of the ordinary to draw attention to himself.

Eli was originally from Argentina. I can only surmise that Argentineans are the most civil people on earth, because I never met a guy who was more courteous or polite. But although he appeared to have adapted with extraordinary ease to life in America he was, it turned out, living a lie; a fact we only discovered on the night of the accident.

Eli had recently opened an upscale dog-grooming salon in Pacific Heights. I personally doubt whether he ever had any actual contact with dogs before arriving in San Francisco, but for reasons known only to himself, he had rented a Fillmore Street storefront, put up a sign, and outfitted his new business with cages, tables, and a wide assortment of stainless-steel dog-grooming devices.

Within the space of two weeks, he was generating enough business to hire a front-desk receptionist and a full-time groomer—someone who actually *knew* how to groom a dog.

Only hours before the accident, we had joined Carol and Eli on a double date at our favorite Greek restaurant. Ever punctual, they had arrived first; and when we walked up to the table, Eli sprang from his chair to greet us. He reached for my wife's hand, kissed it, and then darted around to push in her chair. My wife flashed Carol a self-satisfied smile.

Eli had smooth, olive-toned skin and a wide smile that showed off his white teeth. He was in good shape, too. It was no wonder he was an instant hit with the high-end, mostly female clientele he catered to at his upscale boutique doggie spa.

Dinner was grand. We ordered course after course and drank copious amounts of Ouzo. Two hours later, we were still seated at the table when Eli leaned forward and announced that he had a question he wanted everyone to answer.

"Sure," we replied, ruddy-cheeked and smiling, "what is it?"

"What is the one thing about yourself that if anyone found out, you'd be completely embarrassed or ashamed of?" Eli asked.

Without missing a beat, the three of us exchanged

mischievous glances. My wife began by saying that once, she had stolen a pair of fishnet stockings from a downtown department store, and that the experience had been exhilarating.

Carol slapped her on the arm in mock scolding. I looked at Carol and rolled my eyes. Eli just smiled back mildly at us.

Next it was my turn. "Well, I guess everyone thinks I'm the literary type," I said, "but honestly, the only magazine I actually subscribe to is *Car & Driver*.

A round of laughter erupted from our table. Then Carol added to the hilarity by reminding everyone that I drove a Prius.

Next, Carol confessed that frequently, she wore newly purchased clothes with the tags still on, just in case she wanted to return them later. My wife opened her eyes wide.

Then it was Eli's turn. He was quite drunk by this point, and he rubbed his hands rigorously across his forehead before looking up at us.

"I have a wife and child in Buenos Aires," he said in a halting voice. "They don't even know I'm here...."

The table fell silent. Carol looked over at me, my wife looked at Eli, and Eli just stared down at his empty glass.

"I don't understand," my wife said, breaking the silence. "Why...?"

"I got involved in some drug deals," he replied. "If they find me...."

His voice trailed off. He stood up, bowed slightly to

everyone, and tossed three crisp $100 bills on the table. A moment later, he was gone.

Fortunately, the Rite-Aid was closed that time of night and no one was injured. Eli only ended up crashing through the plate glass window and wrecking the cosmetics counter. A swarm of police was on the scene within minutes.

That night was the last time I ever saw Eli. A week later, Carol told us he was scheduled for deportation. She said that he had called from the county jail the night he was arrested, just to tell her what a lovely evening he'd had, and how very sorry he was that he would not be able to see us again.

Lucky Stars

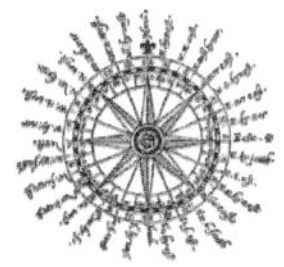

THERE IS a small town up in the California high desert called Lucky Stars. It is the last outpost of human habitation before you enter the dry, rugged wilderness that stretches all the way to Nevada. You head there when there's really no other place left to go— when there's nothing left to explain.

I guess that's why I am closing in on Lucky Stars myself tonight. It's already mid-September and everything runs out in three more weeks—insurance policy on the car, credit cards, foreclosure on the house.

Carla, my wife, left about a month ago, and together with our daughter headed down to her parents' place in the San Fernando Valley. The way I see it, they've cut their losses and abandoned ship. It's not what families are supposed to do, I know that, but I guess we all have our limits—even me.

I've pulled together enough cash to make it a week or two at the Lucky Stars Motel, including meals and a requisite bottle of Jack Daniel's. Who knows, maybe I'll hit it off with a waitress from the local diner. Maybe everyone gets lucky just once in Lucky Stars before they disappear up whatever road it is they're traveling on.

It is nighttime now, and I'm parked high on a hill overlooking the town. I'm reclining on the hood of my car, propped up against the windshield, staring up at the stars. The heat from the engine is keeping me warm against the cool, desert air.

The Milky Way swirls overhead. We're in the middle of that mass of stars, or so I'm told; and beyond that, the constellations print out words in a language that I cannot fathom.

And somewhere back across the hundreds of dusty miles, I was just a regular guy who had backyard barbeques, paid his taxes on time, and sent his kid to public school. But whatever it all added up to just wasn't enough, and when the economy turned bad and my business tanked, we looked around, Carla and I, and we could find no consolation—not from the world, and not from each other, either.

I might like to talk about that a little while I'm up here. Perhaps I'll find someone in Lucky Stars who'll be willing to listen.

There are only two paths you can choose out of Lucky Stars—one leads back along the road you just came from, and the other leads 350 miles across a brittle, barren desert. I'm really not sure which one I'll choose, or when.

Perhaps I'll hatch a new plan while I'm up here

—devise a few options. Or maybe I'll just leave it all up to the stars—they're beginning to fall on me tonight, one after the other, piling up in heaps all around me, spilling out of the night sky.

In the Photo

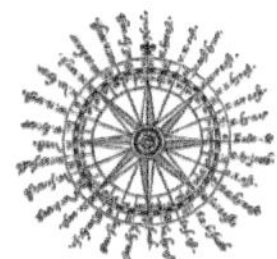

THAT'S ME in the photo, there on the left, standing next to my son. Our proximity is purely accidental, and not solely because we no longer live under the same roof.

It is dusk, and we've just finished eating dinner at one of Timmy's favorite waterfront restaurants. Everything is growing indistinct in the twilight, even Laurie, my second wife. But there she is, camera in hand, determined to capture her perfect father-and-son portrait.

"Tim, move in a little closer to your dad, dear," she says, for about the tenth time.

Tim purposely leans away from me, so that only his waist and torso are in the frame. And each time Laurie edges to the right to gather in Tim's head and shoulders, a part of me slips out of the frame.

"Come on Laurie, for Christ-sakes, let's wrap this up," I say, immediately regretting the angry tone of my voice.

Truthfully, I just don't get people who feel compelled to take photos of every place they go and of every new person they meet. But Laurie, I hate to admit, is just that type.

I have no doubt that she considered this a special occasion, since it's the first time I'm seeing Tim in about six months, and only her second time meeting him at all—but even so, I could really do without the photo op.

My ex-wife tells me that Tim's been going through some stuff since the divorce—at least that's how she puts it. I personally don't remember a time when teenagers "went through stuff" like they do today, but there you have it.

It doesn't escape my notice that I'm not smiling in the picture, either. For one thing, the restaurant was over-crowded, the service was awful, and Laurie wouldn't stop gushing to Tim about the weekend get-away trip we had just made to Aspen.

It may have been new and interesting to her, but I could see that Timmy was brimming with contempt. He knows I never took his mother anywhere. I notice, too, that there's a chiseled look to my own face. I've lost some weight, I'm aware of that, but my face looks as if it has been cast from stone. I don't know where I acquired that joyless look, but somehow, I've grown into it.

But it's my son's face in the photo that grabs my attention. I am looking at him and wondering: what it is that will make Tim happy? Like me, my son has lost his smile.

I turn away from 'Ansel Adams' and look out across the bay. In the distance, I can see several sailboats like white smudges, tilting towards the horizon.

Then, against my will, a warm tear slowly spills down my cheek, a tear that I wipe away with the folded sleeve of my linen shirt—a tear that will not appear in any photo that I'm a part of.

The Way Home

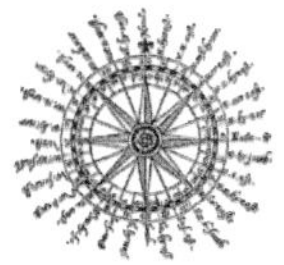

IT IS EASTER SUNDAY and I am standing at the sink washing dishes as I tell you this. For me, doing the dishes often induces a natural state of reverie, like staring into a fire. But Traci, my wife, she has a more pragmatic reason for asking me to do the dishes. At least I have a theory about that.

I am doing the dishes because it's what she instinctively asks me to do whenever she feels threatened by the distance that has opened up between us.

She's no fool. She believes these domestic chores will reconnect me to our house, our family life, and our marriage. It's the kind of intuitive, female knowledge that no "how-to" book would dare to explain.

I have a method for doing the dishes. I begin with the largest plates, wash them, rinse them under the hot water, let them drip for a moment, and then stack them like toy soldiers, one behind the other in the metal dish rack. Next come the smaller plates, then the bowls, then the cups, and lastly, the knives and forks.

Right now, I'm recalling an old picture-book I read and re-read as a child that attempted to teach the laws of gravity to ten-year-olds. I can clearly remember the image of a slim man standing in an open elevator, with the shaft exposed for the viewer, above which, a giant pair of scissors loomed, ready to flex.

'*And*,' the book read, '*if we should cut the cord, dot-dot-dot.*'

The next page showed the hapless man falling through air, his white shirt billowing, and his black tie pointing straight up as the elevator plummeted downwards to certain destruction. Such are the immutable laws of physics.

But the laws of faith offer far more latitude, though their stakes may be equally uncompromising. One can lose faith, come to faith, or even lack faith, but you can be sure the heavenly lawgiver will be far more flexible and forgiving than the authority that presides over falling elevators.

Like my wife and daughter, I, too, went to church this morning—though I didn't tell them I was going. I sat six or seven pews behind them, just watching the back of my daughter's head.

Her chestnut hair was shiny and freshly brushed. A red barrette gathered a small ponytail that swayed a little as she moved; and I saw that like me, she too, was in an in-between place. I just wished I could spare her the pain that I knew was coming her way.

I never thought I would arrive here, at this sad and grown-up place. I recall asking a friend of mine who is also in the process of divorcing his wife: 'Why...what is it about her that's so bad?'

He looked me in the eye and said, "It's not about her, Vic, it's about me. It's about who I'm becoming that I don't like."

When it comes to the ties that bind us, I know of no roadmaps to follow. They say the Magi journeyed to Bethlehem by following a star. All I know is that when you cannot get happy, when you do not know the right road to take, and when you've lost all sense of direction, there is nothing left to do but navigate by stars.

Perhaps, if you're lucky, you'll pass through your darkest night and come out the other side, shedding the tattered cloth of your old self and singing the notes of a new song.

Or, you may just end up like me, doing the dishes and watching shapes of another world that you can see but cannot touch, reflecting back at you from the gleaming dish or shimmering glass drying in the familiar warmth of the kitchen light.

About the Author

Mark Russell Gelade was born in London, England; raised in Montreal, Canada, and is a 30-year resident of San Francisco, where he currently lives with his wife, Colette. He is past winner of The World's Best Short, Short Story Contest, sponsored by Florida State University. His short fiction has appeared in *Narrative Magazine, Southeast Review, Fiction Attic,* and several other literary e-zines. He holds an MA in Poetics from New College of California, where he studied with Gloria Frym, Adam Cornford, and the late David Meltzer. His is currently finalizing a manuscript of poetry titled *Another Life*.

More info about the author is available at:
www.markrussellgelade.com

If you like this book please leave a review on your favorite online bookseller site.

www.ingramcontent.com/pod-product-compliance
Lightning Source LLC
Chambersburg PA
CBHW020534120726

47904CB00003B/1066